DISCARD

Motorcycles: Made for Speed!™

TRICKS WITH BIKES

Connor Dayton

PowerKiDS press™

New York

Published in 2007 by The Rosen Publishing Group, Inc.
29 East 21st Street, New York, NY 10010

First Edition

Editor: Jennifer Way
Book Design: Erica Clendening
Layout Design: Kate Laczynski
Photo Researcher: Sam Cha

Photo Credits: Cover, pp. 1, 11, 13, 17, 23 image copyright Taolmor, 2006. Used under license from Shutterstock, Inc.; p. 5 image copyright Brad Angus, 2006. Used under license from Shutterstock, Inc.; p. 7 image copyright Diane Gonzales, 2006. Used under license from Shutterstock, Inc.; p. 9 image copyright Asian, 2006. Used under license from Shutterstock, Inc.; pp. ; p. 15 © Dan Regan/Getty Images; pp. 19, 21 © Robert Cianflone/Getty Images.

Library of Congress Cataloging-in-Publication Data

Dayton, Connor.
  Tricks with bikes / Connor Dayton. — 1st ed.
    p. cm. — (Motorcycles—made for speed)
  Includes index.
  ISBN-13: 978-1-4042-3657-8 (library binding)
  ISBN-10: 1-4042-3657-0 (library binding)
  1. Stunt cycling—Juvenile literature. I. Title.
  GV1060.154.D39 2007
  796.6—dc22
                                    2006025238

Manufactured in the United States of America

Contents

There are many kinds of motorcycle tricks. Riding on one wheel is called a wheelie.

Spinning a wheel against a **paved** road is called a burnout. It makes a lot of smoke and noise.

Lots of tricks are done up in the air. These kinds of tricks start with a jump.

When a trick is done high in the air, the rider can push off of the motorcycle.

11

A rider might try to stand on the bike as part of a trick. Bike tricks might be **dangerous**, but they are fun to watch.

13

This rider is standing on the handlebars of the bike. This is a hard trick to do.

For some **stunts** the rider will let go of the bike. It looks like this rider is flying over his bike!

Stunt riders who are really good can even do **flips** on their bikes!

People do tricks on all different kinds of bikes. This person is doing a jump on a minibike.

There are games called Stunt Wars, in which riders do tricks for groups of people.

Glossary

dangerous (DAYN-jeh-rus) Might make something hurt.

flips (FLIPS) Turns from head to toe in the air.

paved (PAYVD) Covered with something hard and human made.

stunts (STUNTS) Acts that are hard to do.

Web Sites

Due to the changing nature of Internet links, PowerKids Press has developed an online list of Web sites related to this book. This site is updated regularly. Please use this link to access the list:
www.powerkidslinks.com/motor/tricks/

Index